Miss Dixie and Friends Tails of Survival

Written by Rita Branson Bowman
Illustrated by Tina Modugno

This is Rita Branson Bowman's second book. She lives with her husband Mike and their rescued cats in a small town in Alabama.

This book was written while she was in remission with Non Hodgkin Lymphoma and battling depression. Her wish is that this book will give hope to others. That we all have a will to live and a survival instinct. ALL life matters.

This is a compilation of 13 of Miss Dixie's friends with their true stories of survival and rescues. Told through the eyes of the sweet cats with the help of their rescuers.

I would like to acknowledge the special cat Moms and Dads that shared the rescue stories of their cats and made this book possible.

This continues Miss Dixie's mission that ALL life matters.

Visit Miss Dixie on Facebook:
www.facebook.com/savingmissdixie

Miss Dixie and Friends ~ Tails of Survival

Copyright December 2015 Rita Branson Bowman

ISBN - 13: 978-1519708182
ISBN - 10: 1519708181

Published & Illustrated by Tina Modugno
www.tinamodugno.com

This book is dedicated to my son Dax, who has battled his own demons and survived. I love you to the Moon and back!

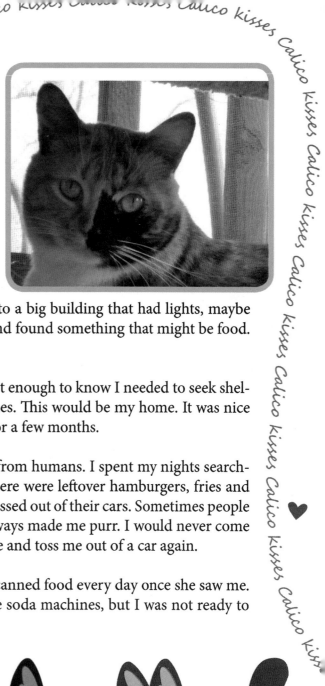

Hi, I'm Miss Dixie and I am a former feral cat. I want to tell you my survival story, and introduce you to several of my friends who have amazing stories to tell. My hope is that by reading our stories of survival it will help you to understand the need for love and compassion for all cats. My story began one night when I was only a little kitten. I found myself tossed out of a car onto the pavement. The car that brought me here sped away, leaving me lonely and scared. I had no idea where I was, all I knew was I was hungry and cold. I ran as fast as I could but I had no idea where I was running. I ran to a big building that had lights, maybe there would be food there. I sniffed around a trash can and found something that might be food. I ate it in one gulp.

That would have to satisfy my hunger for now. I was smart enough to know I needed to seek shelter for the night. I found shelter behind the soda machines. This would be my home. It was nice and cozy. No human could get to me here! I lived there for a few months.

I spent my days behind the soda machines hidden away from humans. I spent my nights searching for food. I found all types of food on the ground. There were leftover hamburgers, fries and chicken pieces. It was amazing how much food humans tossed out of their cars. Sometimes people would leave canned food for me on the sidewalk. This always made me purr. I would never come out from hiding. I was scared thinking they may catch me and toss me out of a car again.

A sweet lady (whom I later called Mommy) brought me canned food every day once she saw me. She tried so hard to get me to come out from behind the soda machines, but I was not ready to trust humans.

5

One night she came and she trapped me in a cage. I was scared, but I knew she loved me. She took me to a Vet where I was poked and prodded. The Vet told me I was now "fixed". All I know is I was so happy to see Mommy when she came to pick me up. I mewed and purred all the way to my new home.

I now live in a big house with seven other rescue cats – all with special stories of survival too.

My life is full of love and my tummy is always full of good food. I play with my rescue brothers and sisters and follow Mommy around the house. I am still scared of humans, even after two years. Mommy says I have come a long way from the scared little kitten hiding behind the soda machines and eating out of dumpsters.

I have my own Facebook pages, a website and a Twitter account. Social media helps me raise money to help many cat rescues. I wrote my first Children's book earlier this year and donated the proceeds to various cat rescues. This is how I help other cats.

After all, the name of my Facebook page is "Saving Miss Dixie and Many More Kitties".

I would like to share the true stories of several of my Facebook Cat friends with you. Each cat has their own story of survival and each one is unique in how they came to be what they are today. They are a true inspiration to all that hear their stories.

Visit Miss Dixie on the web:
www.missdixiesadventures.com

Joe The Cat

Hello, I am Joe the Cat. I once lived in a small apartment with many other cats and a very old man who walked with a walker. We had all sorts of things to climb on because the old man was a hoarder and he was a hermit too. He was a nice man that loved us kitties in his own way. Our tummies were full when bags of food were laid on the floor for us to eat. The old man made a big litter box out of the only bathtub. Most of us had started out on the streets, so a warm place to live was nice.

One day the old man was gone, we never saw him again. Soon, we were all very hungry. We all tried to sleep, but our tummies rumbled from hunger.

After what seemed many sleeps, a strange and angry man entered the cluttered apartment. Everyone scurried and hid, but not me. I went up to the stranger and rubbed against his leg, meowing loud in hopes for food. He was angry with us cats and he kicked me away and began to shoo all of us outside. Some of the kitties had never been outside before and they were very cautious and curious. They were exploring and mousing at first. It was fun for a while... but I knew the fun would end and the hunger would soon set in.

We made the apartment complex dumpster our home. The dumpster could be seen from many of the apartments and some nice humans fed us .

One human sat and watched me a LOT from his second floor apartment. He was a BIG man that looked very mean. He wore a dirty t-shirt that read "I HATE CATS!".

Most of the humans fed us and talked softly to us. I was the friendliest of all of the cats with nice white fur. I would roll over on my back and meow for the humans. They all loved me and called me Dumpster Cat. One lady wanted to bring me inside and be my Mommy – but her roommate hated cats and said "No cats in my house, I hate cats!"

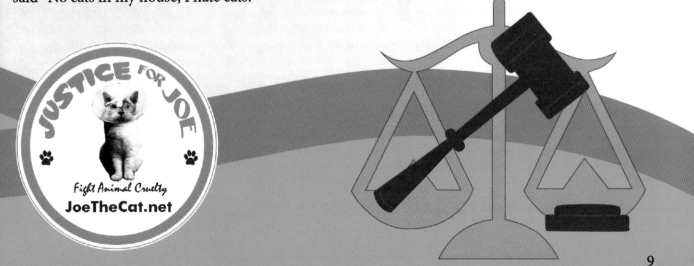

9

I should have been more cautious with people, because, some of them are really mean. One day I went to the apartment looking for the sweet lady that gave me treats. She was not there. Little did I know that there were mean, cat-hating men who wanted to hurt me.

I do not remember much as to what all happened, but I dreamed of my old home, it was a warm place to sleep. I saw the old man and he called to me. "Here Kitty Kitty". I ran to him, but he was gone. Dreams are funny like that.

The cat loving humans came to feed us and noticed I was gone. Dumpster Cat was missing! "Where did the Dumpster Cat go" they asked. They all called out and went looking for me, but I could not hear them. I was nowhere to be found!

It was snowing and very cold – where could I be?

A man in a truck saw something on the side of the road. It was snowing and very cold. He stopped his truck and got out. It was a snow covered lump laying there – then it moved! It was alive!

When I heard the sweet man speak to me, I licked his hand. I knew he would help me. My head hurt so badly. I fell into a deep sleep. But, it was not my time to die. I wanted to live.

The man rushed me to the Vet. This was a Cat Code Red! A team of Doctors and Nurses tried to keep me alive.

"This cat has bullets in his head!" Together the team counted more than 17 bullets in my head. "We will give it our best. It does not look good for this poor cat. He has been exposed for many days, he is dying – but we cannot stop trying!"

After many hours of surgery, I emerged from the operating room with a cone around my neck and a new name- Joe. I was Joe the Cat now. I had many stitches in my head and I had lost an eye – but I was alive!

The sweet man who found me on the road wanted to take me home once I healed. He could not take me home with him because he had a dog that did not want a feline brother. I was in the hospital for a very long time. The man who saved me came to visit many times and I would purr very loud for him.

The nurses loved me the most. They always told me what a good boy I was. And they gave me all the treatz I liked to eatz..! And, they rubbed my belly and scratched my neck all the time.

Meanwhile, the town was reacting with outrage. I was in every paper, on the news, on the internet! I drew attention from people all over the World. People demanded justice for what happened to me.

The World was in love with me – Joe the Cat, a dumpster cat!

While I was healing in the hospital. I was fed wonderful sloppity –slop. The nurses loved to watch me eat and I LOVED to eatz! They kept telling me I was Fayye- Moose. Hmmmm – not sure what kind of moose that is, but they kept telling me that is what I was.

As I slowly healed and grew stronger, so did the Voice of The People. There were protests and petitions. People were very upset and passionate. Joe the Cat's cause was growing. At that time, all I knew was I liked to eatz, I liked the treatz and I liked the belly rubs and neck scratches too!

One day the Vet and Nurses all gathered around me and took a picture. They were crying and I was scared. I wanted to go back to my little room with my treatz. Two humans put me in a car and were driving me away from what I thought was my home.

The humans said "You will have a nice new home with lots of love and food. Your life will be so much better now." And they were right!

Although I do not know what will happen to the mean man who they say tried to kill me, I have found out what Fayye-Moose is! There's two types of Fayye-Moose. Good and Bad. The mean man is the BAD kind of Fay-Moose.

They tell me I am a legend now. I am not sure what a legend is …. Ima cat. Joe the Cat.

A special group of people have kept the fight for Joe the Cat ALIVE! People from all cultures and countries rushed in to show they care with their support and love.

Now, I am now an animal cruelty crusader! While the fight continues and my legend grows, I have a happy life in a wonderful home that has been outfitted for me to go outside safely. My life is good now. I have a big brother Ernie and a little brother Ferb. We wrestle around together all the time. It is so much fun.

AND, Joe the Cat has a partner…. Cat Chance of Sarnia, Ontario.

Cat Chance is a TNR based, rescue, fostering & adoption program. They perform TNR on stray, barn, feral cats. They respond to rescues whenever we can. They have over 65 foster families caring for over 80 cats/kittens up for adoption. Please check out Cat Chance !

As of now.....so much compassion and support continues to be given to Joe the Cat - it is moving to see that one cat's life was worth saving and how people from all over the world cared about a street cat from Sarnia, ON. In doing so, Joe the Cat will remain a beacon for animal compassion. Concerned friends from all over the world united on Facebook, to witness Joe the Cat survive and now, thrive.

The Joe the Cat trial is set for spring 2016. Stay with Joe the Cat.

Visit Joe The Cat on the web: ***www.joethecat.net***

Champy Pants the Blind Siamese Kitty

Hi, my name is Champy Pants! I am a little Siamese kitty who is completely blind and half deaf. My life was not always this way. One day my previous owners in New York City let me out of the house. I think I saw a rat and it was meaty at that! I wanted it so bad and I chased it as it leaped into the street. I did not look both ways and did not see the car coming towards me. I did not have time to escape. Before I knew it, it was just too late! The car drove off and left me in the street.

Then something happened. Someone stopped and picked me up. They took me to a high kill shelter and wished me good luck! There I laid for 3 days in really bad shape. I could not see a thing and I even had a broken jaw. Boy did it ache! I received very little medical attention and was in so much pain. After 3 days of waiting, I was pulled from a local no-kill shelter. I was close to death as they tried for months to save my life. I thought I would be in ICU for the rest of my life. My jaw was wired shut and I got a feeding tube placed in my neck. I lost half of my weight, my eyesight and even became partially deaf!

But then, I started to get better and a friend from far away promised to make my life better. When I was all healed up and ready to go home, my new Mommy and Daddy drove to New York to come scoop me up! I was so excited that I had a new awesome family that would love and even kiss the heck out me! We made the 3 hour drive back to Worcester, MA. That is when I met my new siblings Chewy and Monkey and then Muppet at last!

Since my adoption and new life without sight, my new family assured me my life would be all right! I am now a happy, little blind kitty. I no longer see with my eyes but see fully with my heart. Life is much more beautiful now, than it was from the start!

Visit Champy Pants the Blind Siamese Kitty on facebook:
www.facebook.com/ChampTheBlindSiameseCat

Artist credit: www.cristianbernardini.com.ar

~ Wake up at dawn and put your Champy Pants on! ~

Denver – the CH kitten

Hi, I am Denver the CH kitten. In the summer of 2013, numerous stray cats had been dumped on a rural property in Delaware. The owners of the property fed and tried to spay them all but many were having kittens. My mom was one of them. It was very scary for me and the other babies. There were foxes that would hunt us and one neighbor was threatening to shoot all of us. We were in danger and many of my friends and family were sick. We hid in the bushes and under the house. The owner Kim and her son, Hunter, took all of us kittens and many of the adults into their home to protect us. But, it was too much for the family to handle on their own. They reached out, but no one would help.

Finally, a rescue from Maryland that had heard about the situation reached out to Joa's Arc, a special needs rescue in South Jersey. Joa's Arc tried to get local help for 15 sick kittens which included me, but to no avail. They felt that our only chance was to bring us to NJ. Working with the Animal Welfare Association, Joa's Arc went to Delaware to rescue us. When they arrived back at AWA we were all checked by the vet. I was the only special needs kitten and the vet felt that I would have no quality of life and recommended euthanasia. Joyce from Joa's Arc disagreed and became my foster mom – my Momma Joyce.

I was a happy, spirited little kitten that deserved the chance at a life and they had high hopes that my condition might improve with extra attention and age. My condition was so bad that when I first came into foster care, I couldn't stand, let alone walk. After just a few weeks of extra special care, I showed improvement and was feeling stronger. I even had some acupuncture treatments which also seemed to help. However, it upset me so much Momma Joyce decided to stop taking me. It was possible that I would never walk so she wasn't sure I would ever be adopted.

In October, Momma Joyce took me to a festival event where they had a table to promote awareness about Joa's Arc and special needs pets. This is where I first saw the person I thought would adopt me. However, she had never heard of CH and certainly wasn't looking to adopt another cat. She had 3 big boys at home already. But then it happened! Right after Thanksgiving, she called Momma Joyce and said she wanted to bring me home. Apparently Momma Joyce liked her and trusted her because on December 23rd, she became my Mom too. Mom says I have exceeded everyone's expectations – it may not always be pretty but I walk, I chase my brothers around and I play with my new sister (who also has CH). My life is amazing! I even have my own FB page where I share my daily life and adventures with friends from all over the world. I am one lucky specially-abled kitty!

From Denver's Mom: There is no treatment for CH. These cats do not know that they are disabled and adapt very well. Unfortunately, many are euthanized in our shelters because the shelters are overwhelmed with healthy cats and are unable to care for the special needs ones. We believe that all animals deserve a chance at life and Denver is one of them. He has brought immeasurable joy to my life. His determination and his love of life is amazing.

Footnote: One of the kittens died the day after rescue. It had been shot in the head with a BB gun. The other 13 kittens went to foster homes, were treated for their illnesses and all were adopted.

Visit Denver on Facebook: *www.facebook.com/DenvertheCHkitten*

Frosty The Frozen Kitten

Hi, I am Frosty. My first few weeks of life was in a barn in Wisconsin. It was always cold no matter where I tried to huddle. Snow, ice and harsh winds were all I knew. Food was scarce and I was always hungry. I went to sleep one cold, wet night with my tummy hurting from hunger.
I was dreaming about a Rainbow Bridge and saw my Kitty Mommy and my brothers and sisters playing. I ran to them. Suddenly, they were gone and I was in laying very still in the barn. I realized I was almost frozen. I could not move. My little eyes were frozen open. BRRR.....it was so cold.

One night, a man came inside the barn. He thought I was dead, but he scooped me up and rushed my frozen body over to his neighbor who was a wildlife rescuer. She thawed me out slowly throughout the night.

The next day I was unable to stand, sit or even support myself. She continued to care for me and give me love. She put cream on my ears that were frostbitten. I was such a mess. She talked softly to me and I felt loved. I had a new Mommy and I was so happy.

The next night I saw the Rainbow Bridge again! I was dying. Mommy headed out the door to the Vet. It took her over an hour to get there due to the snowdrifts and white outs. Mommy was so worried. I wanted her to know I wanted to live so I tried to sit upright. She reached over to tell me I was going to be okay and I grabbed her jacket. She put me under her jacket close to her heart and I felt loved. I accidently pooped on her, but she did not mind.

The Vet ran all kinds of tests and agreed with how my Mommy had cared for me at home. They put me in a nebulizer for me to get more oxygen. I responded well with the treatment and everyone was so happy. Suddenly the Rainbow Bridge appeared before me again and I could hear Mommy crying. They placed me in the nebulizer again and added antibiotics. They could tell I was a fighter and I wanted to live! Mommy was given the choice to end my life then or take me to be cared for with a 24/7 Vet.

She rushed me to another ER that offered 24/7 care. They placed me in an oxygen incubator to warm me. I had all sorts of IVs and lines for life support. I stayed in the incubator for 15 days! I was not sure if I would ever come out.

I still have many more months of healing with special treatment for the rest of my life.

I am a happy girl and love to wear sweaters and dresses to keep me warm and I feel sassy when I am dressed.

Mommy said I am still here for a reason. I can give hope to those that feel there is no hope.

I live a wonderful life now and have Yippee – Skippee days because I have a strong will to live.

Visit Frosty on Facebook: *https://www.facebook.com/FrostytheFrozenKitten*

Moses – Crusade of Love

Hi, I am Moses. One of the first memories I have of my childhood is so very sad, sometimes I have nightmares about it. I am in a wet cardboard box, shivering so hard I can still hear my teeth chattering. I am trying to get warm, laying underneath my brothers and sisters. I do not understand why they are not moving around, I cannot hear their heartbeats. Some bad people put us in the wet cardboard box and tried to hurt us. For some reason I did not get hurt, but I knew my brothers and sisters were gone! I start crying, meowing very loudly, praying my kitty mommy can hear me. Nothing!

Then suddenly I heard a soft, loving voice. A human lady pulled me out of the box and quickly wrapped me in what felt like a soft cloud. She tried to see if she could rescue any of my brothers and sisters, but quickly realized they were dead. She took me in her arms, she walked back to her house, later going back to bury my brothers and sisters. She called me Moses and told me I am safe now.

The first year of my life with my first Mommy was very special. I was her only kitty and she spoiled me so much. I really loved to cuddle and sleep with her. She helped me forget how much I missed my kitty Mom and siblings. Then the mean man moved in. He did not like kitties. He kicked me out of the house whenever he had a chance. Sadly, as time passes I see less and less of my first Mommy. What did I do wrong? I missed cuddling and sleeping with her! I did not know that she was growing increasingly ill. When I am a little over a year old, I lived strictly outside. The cold, wet winters were very harsh. I got use to taking cover under the mobile home, curled up in my soft blanket my first Mommy gave me. I was so happy when she brought home Napoleon for me to have a brother. By then I was five years old. Two years later she brought home Spunky. We all had a bond, as brothers should. We all lived outside in the harsh weather. The mean man that lived with our Mommy becomes increasingly cruel to us, even though we were outside. He loved to catch us when we were sleeping and kick us as far as he could. I remember one time when he kicked me. I had a very sharp pain in my hip. I tried to get up. It felt like my bones were rubbing together inside. Unknown to me at the time, he had dislocated my hip. This caused arthritis and would cause pain for the rest of my life. Sadly, Napoleon was the brunt of this mean man's hatred towards cats.

As the years passed, the more I worried about my brothers. The years of abuse and decreasing food took its toll on all three of us, especially poor Napoleon. I calculated I was about twelve years old by then. I came to realize that my first Mommy was very sick and was dying. I decided it was time for me to rescue my brothers and myself. I started going to other mobile homes in the park and looked for a new Mommy, someone who would care for all three of us.

The angels of my siblings must have been watching out for me. It did not take long before I found a really sweet lady that talked to me and began to put food out for me when I came up to her porch. I ate some of the food, but always left food in the bowl, wanting to take it to my brothers so they could eat too. I tried to communicate this to this sweet lady. Each night I tried to get her attention to follow me. I was so happy one night when she did follow me and found poor Napoleon, so very sick from abuse he had sustained over so long and I showed her Spunky in hiding. The sweet lady talked with my sick Mommy and asked if she could please take my brothers and me to her house. The sick Mommy agreed it would be best for us. We were so excited when our new Mommy took us inside her house and told us it was our new home.

We are safe now, with our new Mommy that loves us dearly! Our new Mommy takes care of over 40 stray and feral cats and kittens. But, we know we are the special ones in her life. Life is good.

Visit Moses on Facebook: *www.facebook.com/mosescrusadeoflove*

The Oreo Cat

Hi, I am Oreo. I was abandoned as a small kitten along with my sister. I was found by a nice family that took us home and cared for us. With no Mom cat, my sister and I needed to be bottle fed. While caring for us, the nice family that found us decided to try and find us each a loving forever home.

Our pictures were posted on Facebook by our new human friends. My sister got adopted right away, but she still had to stay with me and the nice family until we no longer needed to be bottle fed. My sister quickly began to grow big and strong. I on the other hand, had very little strength.

A few days after coming to stay with our new human friends, I got really sick and stopped breathing. The nice lady saved me with her very own breath and helped me to start breathing again. I was then brough to the vet where they helped me to feel much better. When I was ready to go back home with my human friends, I was given the most wonderful surprise! The lady and man told me that I was going to live with them forever, and that they were now my new Mom and Dad.

For the next few weeks, my new Mom and Dad did everything they could to help me to feel better. I had a parasite inside of me that they called "Coccidia" and it made me very sick. My Mom and Dad hardly slept at all for the next few weeks that followed. They got up in the middle of the night every night to feed me up until they knew that I was going to be ok. With all of their loving care, I finally pulled through! I am now a happy grown up cat with a big loving family! I have one kitty brother, three kitty sisters, one birdy and one fishy!!

Now a days, I am hard at work helping a wonderful group of people called *The Paw Project*. I help them to teach kids and parents about why cats need claws! Believe me, there are many wonderful reasons! We need them for *protection,* for *exercise,* for *balance* and so much more! Can you think of some good reasons?

To learn more about me, read my books and watch my videos visit: *www.theoreocat.com*

ABOUT THE PAW PROJECT
The Paw Project's mission is to educate the public about the painful and crippling effects of feline declawing, to promote animal welfare through the abolition of the practice of declaw surgery, and to rehabilitate cats that have been declawed. For more information, visit *The Paw Project* website: *www.pawproject.org*

Atchoum The Cat

My life began like a normal Persian kitten born on May 10, 2014 but things quickly changed. I was given as a gift to a veterinarian in Repentigny, Quebec, Canada where my mom, Nathalie works as a groomer. She took me home for a weekend and fell in love with me (no surprise there!). She asked the veterinarian if she could adopt me since I was so adorable. The veterinarian agreed and I found my forever home with two humans, two children and three other cats.

Soon after being adopted it was discovered I have a very rare congenital condition called hypertricosis (also known as werewolf syndrome). It's less scary than it sounds. It means I have a hormonal condition that causes fast and continual hair growth and the thickening of my claws. My claws were growing so large and fast, it was unsafe and I had to be declawed. I also have tiny teeth but that doesn't stop me from eating well. I'm well cared for by a veterinarian who will monitor my health. Since I am the only cat known to have this condition, is unknown how it will progress. Life is good. I feel good and I believe we need to enjoy every day.

It's a good thing my mom is a groomer because my crazy long hairs on my face are thick like a dog. She doesn't over groom me, since she likes my mad scientist look!

So what am I really like? I'm still a kitten so I'm funny like a clown and curious about everything! I'm crazy about the fridge ice machine and run to it every time it makes a sound. Ice cubes and water fascinate me! I love my family and they love me; even when I wake everybody up in the morning by shaking the shower door! I am also very smart! Every time I hear the introduction to a documentary show (that sometimes features animals) on TV (called "Découverte"), I run to catch the animals! I also enjoy playing Cat Playground on the iPad.

My name, Athchoum (which means "sneeze") was given to me because my look is remeniscent of my mom when she sneezes! Since the day that my mom posted my photo on Facebook, I have become widely known all over the internet! I have been compared to many film and book characters because of my unique look! Can you think of someone that I remind you of?

Visit Atcchoum on the web: *www.atchoumthecat.com*

Prince Pippin

My name is Prince Pippin. To be honest, I really do not remember much about my first couple months of life, but I've always been a pretty happy-go-lucky guy with a lot of curiosity! One day, when I was about three months old, I wandered off in search of adventure. I love to explore, and I found a great place to hide, but little did I know I was climbing into the engine compartment of a car! Everything was pretty cool…until we started moving…

You probably know what they say about curiosity and cats -usually it does not end well, but lucky for me, the car was being towed, and at that point, all I could do was hang on for dear life (and enjoy the ride)!

When we arrived at our destination - a car dealership, I made my presence known by MEOWING really loud, like only a Meezer can! When the men opened the hood of the car, there I was, covered with grease and goo to the point they could not even tell what color my fur was! Once again, I got very lucky, because the men that found me were animal lovers, and called a local rescue group, Spay the Strays, the same organization that rescued my brother, Pan Pan. The Rescue came and picked me up, and suddenly I thought "Hey! Wait a minute! Where am I, and where are you taking me?"

The first thing they did was give me a bath. Actually, they gave me several baths, because I was covered in grease. Like most cats, I was not very happy about that, but it was nice to be clean!

Shortly after that, I went to live with my new foster Mom, Ms. Cheryl. She decided to name me Simon. I had a lot of fun at her house, because there was another kitten my age to play with, and of course, lots of great food!

I did not know it at the time, but it was just a few days before Christmas. My future Mommy, in her typical last minute shopping frenzy, had stopped at Petco on the Saturday before Christmas to pick up a new cat tree. Spay the Strays has adoption events on weekends and when a couple of the volunteers saw her in the store, they showed her my photo. She said (of course),"Oh...no, no, no.! I could not possibly get another cat.... Three is my limit!"

They were persistent, however, and talked her into staying long enough for Ms.Cheryl to bring me up to the store. Once I got there, I sat on her lap, and gave her my best purr... I knew I was in! "Well, I'll just tell Daddy you're one of my Christmas presents" she said (she is fond of picking out her own) "Oh, Boy!" I thought, "Off on another adventure!"

I was really looking forward to going to my forever home, but what I did not know was that I would be making a side trip to the veterinarian first (I will not go into what happened there, but you can probably guess)! As promised, my Mommy came and picked me up a few days after Christmas. That was the best gift either one of us could ever receive!

I have a very happy life, and just about everything I could ever want, but I never forget about the cats and dogs out there who are lost, unwanted, injured and alone.

I devote my life to helping organizations, like the one who rescued me, so that someday, their stories can have a happy ending, too.

One last thing... After my first adventure, I am NOT crazy about cars! To this day, I sing the song of my people VERY LOUD, whenever I have to ride in one! But, I still have a great love of adventure! Mew!

Visit Prince Pippin on Facebook: *www.facebook.com/PrincePanpan*

*** *In Memory of my sweet brother Prince Pan Pan – always in our hearts.*

31

Sheldon "chubs"- Broken Jaw Kitty/ love don't abuse animals

Hi, I am Sheldon and my rescue story started back in May 2012. I woke up and I was laying in a ditch. Scared, hungry and covered in fleas. I hurt all over my skinny body. My mouth hurt more than the hunger in my tummy. I do not remember what happened, because it happened so fast. I was knocked out.

I was just a young cat and I had no home. I had roamed the neighborhood for months trying to find food and love. What had I done to deserve this treatment?

I looked up from the ditch and I saw an Angel. She picked me up and saw that my jaw was broken and I am full of fleas – I am a mess. As she carried me to her car, she asked the children that were there what happened. They told her a horse could have done it. I knew that was not the truth, but I could not tell her. Sometimes people are just mean to animals.

My Angel decided she needed to get me to the Vet ASAP. I was shaking so bad, starving and dehydrated. She knew that getting me help was the top priority. I called her my Angel because the rescue that saved me is Pet Angel Adoption & Rescue, Frankenmuth, MI. They called their volunteers Angels and she is a foster Angel.

I do not remember much from my stay, just that I was at the Vet for a very long time. They killed the fleas and fed me. They could not do much about my jaw. The damage had set and they were afraid if they did surgery, it would cause me more pain and it would be very costly for the rescue. So they all agreed since I could eat both wet food and dry, that they would leave my jaw alone. That was ok because I was tired of being in this scary place with all the weird noises, barking, and meowing. One day I heard the Vet people talking about me leaving to go live in a foster home. I was so nervous and excited because I was finally getting out of that cage.

I was at the Vet for about 2 months and finally strong enough to go to a foster home! My foster Mommy-Michelle was so excited to be picking me up from the Vet too. Because I was going to be her very first foster. It was going to be a big day for both of us.

When I saw my Foster Mommy come around the corner, I just knew she would be my savior. She talked to me so kind, and put me in a soft big thing that had wheels. It was pawsome. I could stretch out with so many soft blankies! I was in heaven. I would find out later in my life that it was a stroller and I love strollers! MOL! She talked to me all the way home. She told me about the others at her house. She told me that I will meet Daddy Mike. Most of all, I will meet a very wise kitty name Cody.

When I arrived home, I went through the ordeal of a bath. I was about as filthy as a cat could ever get but I did not fight her. I knew she was helping me.

After trying many names for me, Mommy called me Sheldon and I looked up! Mommy and Daddy's favorite show is "The Big Bang Theory" – thus my name.

I only knew Cody about three weeks before he passed over to the Rainbow Bridge. I was sad that Cody went to the Rainbow Bridge but it gave Foster Mommy and Daddy a chance to adopt me. July 31, 2012, a day I will always remember. This was my adoption date.

I still have to get shots for my mouth, since I am prone to infections. My new Vet counted five breaks that healed, but of course all crooked. I have a canine tooth, about only three others that are half there.

My life is so good now. I have 4 fursiblings that are all rescues like me. One sister named Pepper, four brothers names Stevie Y, CJ (Cody Junior), & Mario. I love car rides. I go to adoption events for local rescues to show that special needs kitties are just as pawsome as regular kitties. I walk with a leash or sit in my stroller. I have been on radio podcasts for special needs and abused furkids. I help with the foster kitties that Mommy takes care of. It makes me happy to teach the kitties new things. Yes, life is good now.

Visit Sheldon on Facebook: *www.facebook.com/Sheldon.Chubs.Brokenjawkitty*

Shadow – A Special Kitten

My name is Shadow, and I live in British Columbia, Canada. This is my story:

My new life began on Friday October 18, 2013. I cannot remember much before that. That day, I was a small kitten, sitting all alone on a little rock in the ditch of a country road. I was loaded with fleas, had worms, and was starving, cold, and badly injured. My left front leg and right front paw were badly mangled and rotting.

I do not remember how I got so hurt or how I got there, but I felt sad, scared, and hopeless. Suddenly, in the distance, I saw a man walking in my direction. He had two dogs on leashes. He was taking them for a walk. I sat quietly, watching them with curiosity. As they got closer to me, the man noticed me. I looked at him but I did not say a peep. He suddenly turned the dogs around and ran back in the direction he came from. I did not know where he went, but after a little bit he came back alone. He had a big box in his hands. He slowly and quietly approached me, speaking softly to me. I was so tired and hurt, I did not run or resist. I just hoped he could help me. He reached down to me, gently picked me up and placed me in the big box. Inside was a warm and cozy blanket. He carried me in the box for a few minutes until we were at a house. The man's wife was there waiting. She had put some wet cat food in a little bowl for me. I hungrily devoured the delicious food. When I finished it, the nice lady gave me more. I could not believe my good fortune. While I ate, I heard the man and lady talking about taking me to something called a veterinarian.

They promptly took me to the veterinarian they talked about. The people there treated me with compassion and said they would help me feel better. The veterinarian was a caring lady who checked me over and gave me some medicine to get rid of my fleas and worms, and tenderly cleaned and wrapped my injuries. The nice man asked if she would be able to fix my injuries. She said I would have to have an operation and she could do it on Monday. I went back with the nice man to his house where he and his wife took care of me, kept me warm and fed, and lavished me with attention.

Monday came and I had my surgery. I was sleeping for the surgery, so I do not remember it. When I woke up, I looked very different. The veterinarian had to amputate my left front leg and part of my right front paw. They shaved some of my fur in order to operate. My incisions were crisscrossed with many stitches. I was very sore but the people there took good care of me. The next day, the nice man and lady came and picked me up and took me back to their home to help me recuperate.

In time, with lots of love and care, I healed. The best part is, the nice man and lady became my Papa and Mama. They gave me a forever home with them and the rest of their fur-babies.

Now, I am a member of a happy family of nine animals (5 cats and 4 dogs) and two humans! I spend my days playing, taking long naps, watching the birds outside the window, and getting love and attention from my Papa and Mama. My belly is full, I have a roof over my head, and I am loved, cherished, and protected. I even get to enjoy my favorite treat - tuna! I am so lucky that my Papa found me that day! October 18th is a day I will never forget - the day I was rescued.

Visit Shadow on Facebook: *www.facebook.com/shadowspecialkitten*

Rasmus Muzmuz

Hi, my name is Rasmus Muzmuz and I am from Denmark. My survival story began when I was a kitten and having a very tough time. I lived in a barn with many other cats and kittens. Food was scarce. We had very little contact with humans.

I ate whatever the big older cats left for us. Sometimes we had nothing to eat and our tummies hurt. We would catch mice and bugs and eat those to survive. We would cuddle together to keep warm at night in the hay. The barn was the only life I had and it was so dirty. It smelled so bad with all the animals that lived in there. There were daily fights between the big cats and we would try to hide to keep from being hurt.

One day we heard the words "hoarders and police". These were strange words, but we knew something was going to happen soon.

The barn where we lived was full of too many cats, and the Police were going to force the hoarders to find homes for us. This scared us all.

One day several strange humans came to the barn. They were trying to catch us. We were all scared and ran. I ran and hid in the rafters of the barn. I would be safe here.

Then I saw a lady looking at me. She called to me and offered me food. My tummy was hurting from hunger. I finally came down to take her food and she took me in her arms.

She told me I was going to live with her now. I was scared but happy to have food in my tummy. I was only 4 months old. My skinny little flea - ridden body had ear mites and I had a bad cold.

My new Mommy showed me so much love and attention. She took me to the Vet and I started on meds to make me well. She gave me toys and food. My tummy had never been full before and this was a wonderful feeling. The best part of my life is all the love and care I now have.

I sometimes have nightmares about my first few months in that barn. Then I wake up, and see my sweet smiling Mommy and I know my life is a good life now.

Visit Rasmus MuzMuz on Facebook: *www.facebook.com/rasmusmuzmuz*

The Daily Pippin

Hi, my name is Pippin. My first memory I have is cuddling with my kitty Mommy and four siblings. My Mommy was a feral cat fed by a nice human. Mommy gave birth to us under a tarp May 3rd, 2011 in the basement. This was a safe place for us all.

One day the human lifted the tarp and saw all of us there. This scared Mommy and she moved us under their deck. This kept us safe from the rain and the heat.

We played and caught bugs and mice. Our feral Mommy taught us to be strong. She was a good Mommy.

As I became older, I began to love the humans. I would cuddle up to them when they brought us food. My brother Goldy did not care for the humans. He liked the food they gave us. He would wait until they left to eat. One other sibling found their forever home and another one passed over to the Rainbow Bridge.

One day, I noticed all of the big feral cats acting scared. I did not know but on August 28th, 2011, hurricane Irene was coming. The rain and high winds were scary. The feral cats were all hunkered down and trying to protect the young ones. Not me! I stayed on the back deck and was getting soaking wet. I was praying I would not drown from the heavy rains. The winds were blowing even harder now, but I stood at the door of the humans. I knew there was safety there. Suddenly the human opened the door and I ran in. I knew I had found my forever home.

Covered in fleas and mud, that is when I had my first experience with baths, 4 baths in 3 days. The fleas left and the humans took me to the vet man after the storm. He said I was in perfect health.

The humans decided I needed a name. They named me after the character in the "Lord of the Rings Trilogy". Pippin was funny and in trouble, and he had a heart of gold. That was a perfect name for me. I soon became the boss of the other kitties in the house. They all look up to me because I have a heart of gold. I take care of my new kitty family and I love my new Mommy and Daddy.

The Daily Pippin

43

Thanks so much to my humans for taking me in from the bad hurricane and giving me my forever home. I still play like a kitten, climb the screen, love my nippy toys and still cannot catch that red dot, but I keep teaching all the newer kitties how to have fun. Feral cats can make the best pets and I am here to prove it. My human Mommy and Daddy take care of the feral colony and I watch them from the windows. Feral life is a scary life and so many do not live a long life. People like my Mommy and Daddy help to make sure the feral cats have food and vet care. The world needs more people like Mommy and Daddy. They know feral cats are good cats and they deserve a good life too.

In 2014 I got my own Facebook page "The Daily Pippin". Check it out and I will show your kitties how to have fun.

Visit The Daily Pippin on Facebook: *www.facebook.com/thedailypippin*

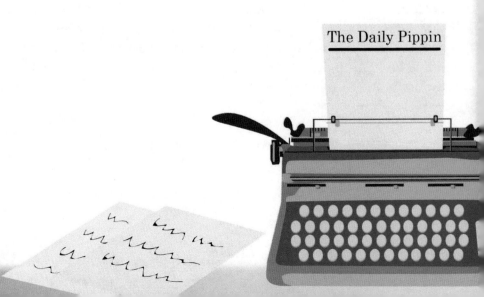

The Daily Pippin

Quirky the Blind Kitten - His Legacy

Quirky was not an ordinary blind kitten...he had a brain and spinal injury that made him blind when he was a baby kitten. We do not know how it happened, it could have been at birth, or from a trauma before he was 5 weeks old. We were told by a Veternarian not to adopt him and that he should be put to sleep. We were already in love with this kitten, and we took our chances. This injury or tumor made his head shake as a kitten, and even though he outgrew it, other symptoms became apparent over his short life.

As he approached his second year, we noticed he never held his tail high like other kitties did, and he walked with his back half downward. His tail was always pointed downward as well. He would not jump up onto anything, so if he could not climb up somehow, he could not get up onto anything.

As his two year birthday approached, he became increasingly fearful of his world. Before this time, we could always pick him up and cradle him in our arms, belly up, and calm him immediately. This ceased to work. We would find him in the middle of a room 'looking' up and screaming in terror. When we picked him up he would growl and shake. As this happened more frequently, he just died one morning.

His legacy for everyone is to have you know how loving and trusting blind kitties are. They see nothing to be afraid of so they have no fear. Quirky was a fearless little kitten. When I picked him up at the shelter he went limp in my arms and fell asleep. He knew he was safe. He was also more loving than one would think a cat could be. He would snuggle in my arms at night curled up between my arms and knees with his head on my arm as I lay on my side. With my other hand, I rubbed his ears while he purred us to sleep. He would lay there all night. When I would wake up I would stretch out one of his little arms and rub it all the way up to his toes. I rubbed each one of his toes as he stretched them out. We would do this every night. I do not think that an ordinary cat would have stood for this kind of cuddling. He would just absorb all the love you could give him and radiate it right back. I think this is one of the most amazing qualities of a blind kitty.

Quirky would have wanted you to tell the world how amazing blind kitties can be, and he would have wanted all blind kitties to be adopted and not discarded, put to sleep, or left at shelters. If you want the experience of a lifetime, please consider adopting a blind kitty. If you cannot adopt one, spread the word. Each one of us can help them get adopted.

Please help Quirky's Legacy...it is his gift to you.

Visit Quirky on Faceboook: *www.facebook.com/Quirky.theblindkitten*

Visit Miss Dixie on Facebook: *www.facebook.com/savingmissdixie*

Visit Joe The Cat on Facebook: *www.facebook.com/JoeTheCatSarnia*

Visit Champy Pants The Blind Siamese Kitty on Facebook:
www.facebook.com/ChampTheBlindSiameseCat

Visit Denver the CH Kitten on Facebook: *www.facebook.com/DenvertheCHkitten*

Visit Frosty the Frozen Kitten on Facebook: *www.facebook.com/FrostytheFrozenKitten*

Visit Moses Crusades of Love on Facebook: *www.facebook.com/mosescrusadeoflove*

Visit The Oreo Cat on Facebook: *www.facebook.com/TheOreoCat*

Visit Atchoum's Fan on Facebook: *www.facebook.com/AtchoumsFan*

Visit Prince Pippin on Facebook: *www.facebook.com/PrincePanpan*

Visit Sheldon "chubs"- Broken Jaw Kitty/ love don't abuse animals on Facebook:
www.facebook.com/Sheldon.Chubs.Brokenjawkitty

Visit Shadow a Special Kitten on Facebook: *www.facebook.com/shadowspecialkitten*

Visit Rasmus MuzMuz on Facebook: *www.facebook.com/rasmusmuzmuz*

Visit The Daily Pippin on Facebook: *www.facebook.com/thedailypippin*

Visit Quirky the Blind Kitten - His Legacy on Faceboook: *www.facebook.com/Quirky.theblindkitten*

Made in the USA
Charleston, SC
12 February 2016